KNEE DEEP *in* LITTLE DEVILS

A Write or Die Anthology

Edited by
Karen Yun-Lutz

Copyright © 2018 by WorD Publishing-pgh. All rights reserved. No part of this publication may be reproduced, distributed, or transmitted in any form or by any means, including photocopying, recording, or other electronic or mechanical methods, without the prior written permission of the publisher, except in the case of brief quotations embodied in critical reviews and certain other noncommercial uses permitted by copyright law. For permission requests, write to the editor at: editor@wordpublishing-pgh.com

First paperback edition October 2018

Front cover illustration, "Yellow King in Carcosa," by: Rhonda Libbey
Back cover illustration, "Dancing with Demons" by Nancy Farmer
Book and cover design by Karen Yun-Lutz
Chapter illustrations by Kevin M. Hayes and Jesse Lutz

Library of Congress control number: 2018903524

Created in the United States of America

10 9 8 7 6 5 4 3 2

ISBN-13: 978-1-7320799-0-8
ISBN-10: 1-7320799-0-0

Dedicated to
Chris Von Mayendorf
For believing in us, and this project.

CONTENTS

FOREWORD

I'm glad you've decided to join us on this strange journey. How strange is it, I hear you ask? It was so strange that we made a book out of it. But you already knew that, because here it is firmly in your grasp. Since we're both here, I would like, if I may, to tell you the story of how this book came to be. Or at least my version of it.

So where shall I begin? With that night? That is always a wicked place to start--especially if you're looking for a frightfully good story.

Okay, here goes. Eleven authors, nine Stories, two Poems, and seventeen Haiku walked into a bar . . . actually, I'm pretty sure it was a bookstore, but I'm getting ahead of myself. Let me start again, this time at the very beginning.

It was a dark, stormy night, around Halloween, which happened to be in October again that year. Which was fortunate for our revelers, for any other night of the year might not suffice. Which was also a night when all the goblins were out hooting, carrying on, creating a ruckus and causing devilish mayhem, and drivers were trying to avoid killing the little goblins that were running amok in the streets. (did you notice the three whiches? Just like MacBeth and Hocus Pocus!)

The revelers in this story didn't get out often. Sad but true. But on this particular night they were out. I expect someone had accidentally left the door unlatched and they escaped the confines of their dwellings. Jacked-up like rabbits during mating season, they bounded into the night to join their friends and look for frights. Little did they know, the frights would find them!

Pumped-up on sugary snacks, the revelers entered the bookstore just in time. (The book store is one of those aged ones, crammed tips to toes with tomes on everything from Adams to Zelazny. The dim lighting is perfect for losing yourself among the stacks as you wander from row to row, listening to the voices of the dead scream from within the dusty pages. I believe this particular store still exists, but I haven't had the courage to visit since that fateful night.)

The boisterous revelers, intent on enjoying an amusing evening of author readings and refreshments, found seats and settled in. (Many of them were the authors of the stories that were scheduled to be read, which is why they were so stoked.) The first reader stepped up to the mike and the event was underway! What our fine participants didn't know was that an unseen force was at work that night. I believe we all felt it, but were too excited to give it much thought. It was only when the master of ceremonies called the name of the thirteenth reader, did he notice his audience seemed a bit sparse. One of the authors sitting in the back row of the audience heard shuffling sounds coming from deep within the rows of books and mentioned it to the remaining guests. The MC, hell-bent on having the full attention of everyone; audience and participants alike, went to investigate and hopefully coerce his audience back to their seats.

Moments later the the shuffling sounds grew in volume and in proximity to the audience seating area. A sudden chill spread through the room as a high wind shrieked outside and shook the huge windows of the bookstore. The lights went dead. Let me be frank with you, I was filled with so much terror that I bolted for the door. I was the first and only one to make it out the door. (Being a long-time Stephen King/Dean Koontz/Clive Barker/JD Barker fan, I understand on a very deep, personal level, how this works). I watched from outside, through the perceived safety of the thick plate glass. (So call me a wuss. I deserve it. But, I'm alive to tell this tale.) I watched as the missing authors, guests and the MC, shuffled out from between the rows of bookshelves. Ghastly white-faced, they reached for the remaining audience, who were frozen in fright in their seats—or maybe they were too inebriated on fine mead to care. Who knows.

I can't describe what happened next because I didn't see what happened. (Seriously, I didn't!) At that very moment, a tremendous blast of lightning hit the store followed by a deafening peal of thunder that shook the building. The sound rolled into the night like the beat of a distant tom-tom. Everything went dark. I must have passed out. (How convenient, right?) When I came to, laying on the cold sidewalk outside the store, I was soaking wet from the torrential rain. Anxiously got to my knees and peeked in through the window. The author-revelers and the remaining audience were gone. All of them. Not a soul was in sight. Not even the bewitching shopkeeper.

I crept into the dark store, deciding to have a look around to make certain no one was in need of assistance. Distant chirrs, similar to the sounds katydids make, only much creepier, caught my attention. The sound repeated. Several times. Ominously. I took a deep breath, steeled myself for the worst and set out to search the shadowed rows of books. (So maybe I'm not a complete wuss. Of course I had my cell phone flashlight to illuminate a small distance ahead of me, so that helped.) I felt a slight touch, first on one shoulder then the other; as if a light wind had blown across my back. Spooked, I jumped, let out a pitiful yelp and turned to look. There was no one behind me. Cold chills ran up my neck and down the backs of my legs. Every fiber of my being wanted to turn and flee from the store— screaming. But those revelers were also my friends. I wasn't leaving without searching for them. Deep in my gut I knew that there was no hope of ever finding them, but I had to at least try. Finally giving up (after searching for about two and a half minutes), I headed for the the front of the store. I glanced around one last time—just to make absolutely sure I wasn't leaving anyone behind.

They were standing . . . right . . . behind me. All of them! Unmoving and silent, their slack faces ghostly pale, limp arms hanging loose at their sides. (Wherever you are, reading this, I suggest you check behind you. There might be someone standing behind you, watching. Their breathing shallow enough that if you listen carefully, you can just hear the small sound of their breath as they exhale.)

And who was leading the slack-jawed revelers? Larry. I shoulda guessed. His shiny silver hair was pulled up into a full man-bun. He stood at the front of the group; always a leader when it came to new trends—and apparently even zombification. Everyone dug Larry.

Now he just looked like someone needed to dig a grave *for* him. He took one lurching step forward; one outstretched, ashen hand reaching for me. I stumbled backwards, tripped over a folding chair and landed on my ass. Hard. (It really hurt!) Scrabbling to my knees, I reached for a shelf of knick-knacks and sent the shelf (and all the little odities, crocheted critters and whatnots) crashing to the floor. At last, I regained my footing, turned and raced towards the door like the hounds of hell were on my heels. As I passed the podium I snatched up the stack of manuscripts and ran from the bookstore. I didn't stop running until I reached the safety of my home--where I compiled the stories and poems into the book you now hold in your hands.

I'm not going to try to convince you that this is the unvarnished truth. You either believe my story, or you don't. All I know for sure is that it took a lot of courage for the writers to attend that first event and stand in front of a group of their peers and read their stories. And it's fortunate that I got out just in the nick of time. The Write or Die group is a great bunch of people and I'm gratified that I get to be a small part of it. I've watched many of the members grow from emerging writers to published authors.

If I may, I would like to throw in a little backstory on how the second inception of the Write or Die group was started. In May of 2012 Kevin Hayes and I started discussing a reboot of the Write or Die group. The first group just kind of faded out after a long run and had been defunct since June 21, 2011. It took some planning to get the new group up and running. First thing we needed to do was to find a business (preferably a bookstore) to host the meetings.

After eight months of planning, we officially held our first meeting on January 29, 2013 at the bookstore that was then called Eljay's Used Books. The store changed owners in the summer of 2013 and six months later the name was changed to Rickert and Beagle Books. Six people showed up for the event and Kevin was ecstatic. We both missed the in-person, social writing camaraderie that the WorD group provided.

In 2014 the topic of public author readings was brought up during one of the regular meetings. Oh yes, we discuss all aspects of writing during the meetings. Many of our members at that time were emerging writers and many of them had never been asked to do a public reading. My first public reading back in 2005 is a huge, black gaping hole in my memory. I was so completely terrified that I don't remember it. As a new author, I never imagined I would be asked to stand up in front of real human beings and read my work. (shivers) This gave me the idea to start a reading event where our members could read their stories in a safe and comfortable environment. Halloween seemed like the perfect time to combine a party of sorts, with a frightful reading event. The first Halloween Reading event was also a challenge. Members who wanted to read for the event had to write a Halloween-themed story in less that two weeks that could be read in under ten minutes. The event was held on Oct 28th. Ten WorD members and four guest authors came out to read. We opened the doors to the public, held a raffle and had refreshments. The event was so much fun that we decided to hold it annually.

This anthology is a direct result of the first three Halloween Reading Events. The stories contained herein are stories that were read during those first three events. All of the authors donated their stories to make this anthology become a reality. I am gratified that they believe in me enough to entrust me with their their treasured words.

The new Write or Die group still follows many of the same rules and procedures that were set up for the original group. We hold regular writing and critique meetings at Rickert and Beagle Books every-other Tuesday from 6:45-9:00 pm. Meetings are free to attend and open to the public. Our schedule can be found on our website, www.word-pgh.com

And now that I've told this story, I'm going to go get myself a nice, hot cuppa Joe, relax and enjoy the stories the Write or Die authors produce. I hope you'll join me.

~Karen D. Yun-Lutz, editor

(P/s You did check behind you. Just to be sure. Didn't you?)

Eat too much candy
you will get a stomach ache
broken glass inside

-*Vincent Baverso*

A CHECKUP FOR MR BANGLES

by Michael A. Arnzen

"Daddy, Mr. Bangles is dying."

I dropped my magazine onto my lap and saw Cindy holding her doll up toward me. I smiled at the little cutie pie.

"Dying? What ever gave you that idea?" I took her offering and propped the doll up on the arm of my recliner. It weighed about as much as Cindy did a few years ago, when she was in diapers. But Mr. Bangles' hard plastic was nothing like a child's pudgy flesh. I examined his face and his plastic eyes rolled to the left, looking askance as they always did -- a weird directionless gaze that made him appear as if he'd just committed some petty toybox crime. A stupid doll, as far as they go, but Cindy loved him. "Mr. Bangles looks as chipper as always."

"I don't think so, Daddy." Cindy leaned her sharp little elbows on my knees and cupped her chin her hands. "Look at his face. He don't look good. I think he's gonna die soon."

Cindy's morbid thoughts troubled me. I thought she had come to terms with the concept of death after our long talk about it when she'd discovered Kitta Katta in a pile of fur and flies in the cellar last year. She was depressed for about a week, but cheered up quickly and hadn't spoken about it since. Yet clearly she was still processing the whole idea that nothing lasts forever, because here she was, presenting Mr. Bangles as if she wanted me to ward off her fears.

So I pretended to examine Mr. Bangles the way a doctor might, going through the motions of a check-up, just to reassure her. And maybe invite her to talk it out, if she felt ready.

I pulled up his plastic eyelids with my thumbs, leaning forward to peer into his eyes. "His eyes look good," I said as I squinted to look into his glossy white ball bearings. "No pink eye or impetigo," I added, knowing that Cindy had experienced a bout of conjunctivitis just last year.

A doubtful *hmm*, was all she said in reply, but I could tell she was enjoying this attention, having successfully gotten me to play with her and her dolly.

I twisted Mr. Bangles' head away from her, till his chin was impossibly positioned over his neck. "Now cough!"

I didn't grab between his legs, but the idea of doing a testicle check made me laugh a little. The laugh barked out of me, but I kept my lips closed and camouflaged it by doing a little ventriloquism, emulating a coughing sound in the back of my throat.

Then I turned Mr. Bangles' melon-sized head to face Cindy directly. His eyes swiveled a little inside the sockets when I twisted his neck, and then they settled in a way that fell directly in the path of her gaze. "I think Mr. Bangles here is just fine."

Cindy twisted her cheek to lean on one palm. She smelled like watermelon candy as she puffed out her breath and rolled her eyes up at me. "You didn't check his tummy." She blinked, her own wide and shiny eyes a little doll-like too.

I pulled Mr. Bangles' checkered shirt up to reveal his plastic belly, and found the presence of a plastic "outie" button. His flesh felt a little disturbing beneath my fingers as I pressed here and there, imitating how doctors had examined my own stomach before, feeling for god knows what during the routine check-up.

"He feels fine," I said to her, even though the hard-yet-rubbery plastic of his inhumanly thin skin did not feel fine at all. It reminded me of the feeling of my wife's kangaroo-like belly, when she was pregnant with Cindy five years ago. I even detected what might have been heat. And when I pressed harder, I could hear air hissing out from somewhere else in his body -- a slight farting whisper that I imagined very well might be coming out of his "just atomically correct enough to fool a five year old" body.

"Is he okay?" Cindy asked, breaking my concentration. She might have caught me frowning as I felt around the doll's stomach with growing concern.

"Umm...I think he might have a little tummy ache," I said, pressing more gently with my fingertips. "Nothing a little cup of tea can't help."

She had played tea time with Mr. Bangles almost daily. Maybe she'd run with my idea and go play with him and let me get back to my magazine.

"Check his heart!" she burst out, letting go of her head and jumping away, heading over toward her children's tea table nearby.

I placed a hand over the center of his chest, but hesitated. For some reason, I was dead sure I was going to find a pulse. I looked into Mr. Bangles' eyes. They stared at the floor like a dead man's. Surely I was imagining things.

I laid my hands upon his crumpled checker shirt, guessing at the spot between where his dolly nipples might be located. At first I was relieved to discover nothing but hard plastic torso. But as I pressed down, I realized my fingers were sinking a little. I adjusted my position. Felt hard edges. A dampness. I lifted his shirt all the way up. A ragged hole was cut into the plastic, revealing a meaty red interior.

Cindy interrupted my disgust with a second horror -- a tea cup she positioned under my eyes -- red liquid brimming like soup over a gory muscle dumpling. "Can you check it? I think it broke when it came out."

An earthen decay
a perfume of dying leaves
the scent of autumn

-Vincent Baverso

A WALK IN THE PARK

by Frank Oreto

It was dark. Not late, only 9:30, but very dark. I decided to walk home. It would be scary. *That* was the whole point.

October was winding down, almost time for Halloween. The time of cool nights and falling leaves. A time to try to recapture the thrills and chills that came so easy when I was a boy. A time to be scared.

No better way to start things off than a night walk through the park. I had my phone, that modern security blanket we all carry, but the charge showed only a hair-thin sliver of red—perfect. A sign near the path read ONE WAY. The arrow pointed back in the direction I'd come. It wasn't "Abandon all hope ye who enter here," but I tried to take it as a bad omen.

Fear does not come easily to a white, middle-class guy in his forties. Worry sure; cancer, money problems, my kids. I could worry most people under the table. But what I wanted was fear. I had to coax it.

I conjured up the scariest thing I could imagine. A blood-drenched child sitting on a swing. Not in the giant well-lit wooden play area, but on the bigger swing-set further up the park's slopes, all by itself. The child swung slowly back and forth staring at me. Every parent's nightmare, an innocent violated, or maybe something worse, something feral and dangerous, considering its next victim.

Horrible? Yeah, and effective. Gooseflesh sprang up along my arms.

The image dissipated as quickly as it came. It was too Hollywood. Right out of a Nightmare on Elm Street. But the fear lingered.

I did not have to reach for dread anymore. The night took over the job. The park was full of the kind of trees whose bark peels away in strips, exposing wood the color of yellowed teeth. The leaves were dry and gave the wind a harsh, rasping voice. There were streetlights, but only a few. I had to cross through pools of ink-dark shadow to get from one to the next.

My back tingled. Why? Because there was someone behind me. Was there really? I didn't know. I couldn't look back. If you look back, that's when those extra footsteps, the ones you keep telling yourself are echoes, speed into a run.

The rasping wind whispered its threats and tree branches reached toward me with the languid slow motion of undersea plants. Every object more than ten feet away grew ominous. The shapes just indistinct enough to allow my mind to play with them, to form them into things befitting the occasion.

My flesh crawled. It's a weird sensation. Some people go their whole life without experiencing it. It really does feel like your skin is moving—a slow wave of tightening derma, creeping up the nape of your neck on its way to the top of your skull.

I walked faster, letting out a pent up breath each time I reached the false safety of the next light. To my left, down a steep grass covered slope, I heard the distinct hyena-laughter of teenagers. The red eyes of their cigarettes stared up at me from dark silhouettes.

I was almost out now. I walked through shadows toward the last of the park's lights. Dammit it, it was too soon. I wanted the feeling to go on at least a little longer. Just let me be that kid again, shaking under the blanket, knowing despite what my mom told me, the bogeyman did exist. He was huge and twisted, had claws and sharp teeth. And he was right there, right beside me.

I stepped into the light. People were coming down the path—a man my age. He could have been me. Dark hair, balding but not succumbing to a comb-over yet. His wife, a stout woman with the same dark hair, accompanied him. A tall boy with a crew cut completed the nuclear family. The solid boring reality of them, of me, ripped through my carefully crafted dread.

I hated them a little. I hated the fact that I had grown up and lost some of myself along the way. I wanted to yell BOO and run into the night laughing maniacally, but of course I didn't. Instead, I nodded at the dad. "Evening."

He gave a response and raised his hand to cover up a yawn. Still wrapped up in my own thoughts, I only half heard his words.

Finally, I strode out of the park onto the sidewalk proper. All and all the walk had been exactly what I needed. I turned and took a last look back.

The family of three was there, but they were stepping off the pathway, out of the light, heading down the dark slope where the cigarette-smoking teenagers had laughed. They moved differently now, hunched over, their arms hanging low at their sides. There was something wrong with their heads. The backs of their skulls had grown huge as prize-winning pumpkins. As I stared, the man looked back over his shoulder. His head turning so far I expected to hear the snap of bones. His face was a steep slope leading down to a lantern-sized jaw. Our eyes locked, and just before the shadows took him, he smiled.

I saw that smile and my stomach dropped as if I had gone over the first big hill on a roller coaster and never stopped falling.

What had he said to me on the path, before yawning and covering his mouth? (You should always cover your mouth when you yawn because it's the polite thing to do, or maybe because you don't want anyone to see all those needle-sharp teeth, at least not until later, when you smile). I had heard him. I just couldn't recall the words.

I'd been too busy trying to hang on to those last tendrils of false fear.

A scream rose from the park, then another. There was a shouted obscenity. The voice high and broken. Then the cries cut short, the way a strong hand smothers a bell.

That sudden silence was my trigger. I finally got what I wanted. The pure terror of childhood filled me, hot, huge and beyond any doubt. I hadn't lost the feeling after all. A younger wiser me had walled it away. I'd replaced it over the years with a nostalgia-drenched cartoon version of dread. But the real thing still screamed behind the bricks. Clawing at itself, waiting to be set free.

I ran. My house was still three blocks away. How long before the man and his family finished with the teenagers? My flesh crawled again. My skin beaded with goose bumps.

I remembered now what the man had said, on the well-lit path, before he stepped into the shadows and became something else. I wanted to forget those words, I wanted to go back to being a grown up, where I was in control and being scared was a once a year novelty. But my childhood fear was free at last and it howled the man's words like some demented mantra.

"See ya soon. See ya soon. See ya soon."

Trick or treating kids
knocking on the witches door
sweet treats delivered

-Vincent Baverso

A STORYBOOK HALLOWEEN

by Kevin M. Hayes

It was the kind of Halloween everyone remembers from the stories they read as children--gloomy and forbidding, chilly and startling. Heavy clouds scudded across the stygian sky, covering and uncovering the bright disc of the full moon. Shadows of web-decorated trees and bushes danced a macabre tarantella in the dark and secret places on the street. And I'm sure I overheard more than one parent swear to their six-year-old they were positive they had just seen a witch flying on her broom before the wind, ripping across the face of the darkness. Things happen on a Halloween like this. That's why I was out in the first place. I thought I was doing my job--well, not really a job when you consider that it's all volunteer. That's the way a Neighborhood Watch works--it's volunteer. My grandmother started our watch back in the '60s, just before she died. My family and the neighborhood have kept it going ever since. Even Lindsay, my daughter, texted me that she wished she could get back to help, but school was just too far.

A mom out with her two sons, Diane Stilson, yelled at me from two houses away and roused me from my reverie. "Dimitri! 'Dja see that kid? Over at Rialto's? She looks kind of lost"

I looked down the street following the direction of Diane's pointing finger. The little girl was there, at the edge of Hank Rialto's yard, peering around the huge foam-core headstones and watching fake fog roll in waves over the heads on pikes. There was also a flying ghoul that would reach a point, whirl in one direction, then seemingly unwind and whirl in the other. Usually Hank has a great Halloween display, but this year it was like he had tried too hard. The man, himself sat on his steps, dressed in an old-style baseball uniform, drinking beer and muttering to himself.

When the girl saw me heading down the street towards her, she glanced over her shoulder, then back at Hank. Then she ran into the street and came to meet me half way. The girl couldn't have been any more than nine or ten. At least that's how she looked to me. A great age for trick-or-treat and Halloween.

"Are you okay here?" I asked. I looked at her costume. She had a Little Red-Riding Hood cape with the hood pulled up. Under the cape, she had a blue pinafore dress, knee-socks and Mary Janes. The cape seemed a little ragged, like it had been torn by something

"I don't know. Do you see it?"

"Do I see what?"

"The wolf. He's been after me all night."

I rocked back on my heels and peered around. "Nope, no wolves around that I can see. Are you out with anybody else? Some friends maybe, or your mom or dad?"

She appraised me for a moment. Maybe she was older than the nine or ten I first took her for, or maybe just a little more street-wise than most. I suppose she decided I was okay. "Mom's at home passing out the candy and Daddy's not feeling well. So I came out by myself."

"So, not even friends? Cousins? Other neighbors?"

"Nope. None of my friends wanted to come over here even though everyone knows they're the best trick-or-treat streets anywhere."

"Well, thanks. We like to think so. My name is Dimitri, welcome to our neighborhood." I looked around for a moment for someone else to take a hand with this child. Hank was no good, Diane had her hands full with her two and she was talking with Arielle and Jack Rankin. There were some others still out, but they were all busy with their own crews. Me? I just keep an eye on the festivities anymore; the job of the Neighborhood Watch, right?

"Well, shoot. What's your name, sweetie?"

"Lucy, Lucy Hanover."

"If you'd like, I can walk with you for a while, till you decide you've had enough trick-or-treating. And then make sure you get home okay."

She started to answer then stopped. "Did you hear that?"

I listened--nothing but kids, some sound effects coming from one of the spooky front yards and the slight wind soughing through the trees. "Sorry, sweetheart, I don't hear anything unusual."

"No, you gotta really listen, please!"

When I managed to ignore all the other typical Halloween sounds, I heard it. It was a panting, a puffing--like what you would expect from a large dog. I looked at her.

"You heard it, didn't you?" Her face took on a serious intensity. "Tell me."

A low groaning wail, just loud enough to be eerie, raised the hairs on the back of my neck. "I hear it. Probably Flaherty's Great Dane. He can sound pretty scary sometimes."

A rustling came from some bushes across at the Peterson's, followed by what looked like a pair of red eyes reflecting the meager street lights, gazing at us from the depths. More panting emanated from the trembling tight-grown branches and leaves. When I focused on trying to make out what was concealed in the foliage, the panting gave way to a low, throaty growl.

I backed away, still watching the shrubs at the Peterson's and took Lucy by the shoulder. "Well, maybe now would be a good time for us to get you safely home. Where do you live?"

I took Lucy by the hand and backed up a few more steps, then turned and strode quickly away, hoping to put some distance between us and the bushes. Lucy kept up.

"Over on Plymouth. Near Edgerton."

"Wow, you really <u>did</u> come a long way for Trick-or-Treat, didn't you? Well, if it comes to it, the Police Station is between here and there, and my grandmother's house--well, it's my house now; that's even closer. We'll find you somewhere safe." I offered her my hand and she took it. We kept walking--fast.

I could hear the clicking of claws on pavement, but I worried that turning to look would slow us down. I risked a quick glance over my shoulder and saw a dark rangy lupine body disappear into Halloween decorations on someone else's lawn.

Being pursued by something you fear may kill and eat you brings a certain intense awareness of your surroundings. The dark was rife with sounds and smells I had ignored until now. I was using every heightened sense I could summon to stay alert to our goal and our pursuer. I could hear my own breath in my ears; I heard Lucy gasping as she struggled to keep up. The sounds of the beast as it moved from place to place following us didn't seem hurried. It didn't run; it was stalking us. We had been singled out as the prey and it was waiting for us to tire.

A sudden movement seen in the corner of my eye and the animal had grabbed Lucy's cape. Her shrill scream had an odd double effect. It moved me to action and stunned the attacking carnivore. It froze, holding the red material taut, as if waiting for the little girl to collapse. I wrenched her away from the monster and kicked it in the throat with my heavy boots. Ten years of martial arts training does come in handy.

Four houses away from my house. I knew we wouldn't make it to her home, much less the Police Station if the wolf had anything to do with it. But we could make it to mine. The animal stood no more than ten feet away, head low, a snarl on its lips. It peered at us, watching, waiting for another chance to attack. Its chest heaved with every breath. I could smell the foulness that surrounded this creature; I sensed the evil intent. This animal wasn't crazed, it was calculating. It leaped, lunging at me again; I sidestepped, grabbed it by the fur on its neck and used its own momentum, throwing it into a snare of spider web-strewn yard decorations. The harder it struggled with the stringy ornamentation to turn and attack again, the more entangled it became.

I seized Lucy's hand as I ran past. We had to move before the beast freed itself from the encumbering fibrous net. A howl of frustrated anger split the night. It was only four houses; we could sprint that far, right? We pounded down the street. My lungs burned, Lucy's face was red in the moonlight from the exertion. Perspiration made my hand slippery and I lost my grip when she tripped as we hurdled the curb into my yard. She went under my feet and we both screamed as we fell. Even in my panic, I could hear the loping claws on the street, the fetid bellows-breathing of the monster. I grabbed a zombie arm from my own Halloween décor as it leaped at me and forced the rubber and steel appendage between the tooth-filled jaws. It ripped the shielding limb from my grasp and shook it. I crab-walked away from the dark-furred demon. Lucy was already at the door, hauling it open and diving inside. I was across the yard and into the house behind her with the wolf at my heels.

I leaped through the door only to be tripped by Lucy's extended leg. I tumbled into the entry and lay sprawled on the floor as the wolf jumped into the open doorway.

"Now, Daddy, now!" Lucy screamed and slammed the door to face me. Glowing with triumph, her eyes held the same red, feral fierceness as the wolf's.

As the wolf leaped at me, a sharp silver knife flashed across the space, pinning the attacking beast to the wall.

My grandmother stepped from the shadows into the moonbeams illuminating the room from the front window. She looked as beautiful as ever, pale, young, eternal.

"Ah, Dimitri," she said. "You always bring me such wonderful treats on Halloween." Her fangs glinted in the moonlight.

Some lingering souls
still occupy this household
evicted tenants

-Vincent Baverso

FROM THE DEEP
by Larry Ivkovich

On this All Hallows Eve, I see everything so clearly. At long last I, Alanlla Steadman, know who I really am. How fitting this knowledge, this glorious affirmation, should occur on the night when the veil between worlds is at its weakest and most accessible.

Dream-images of a wondrous undersea realm envelop me in a powerful, familial embrace. My rightful lineage hidden since birth, I'm held enthralled by the startling reality revealed in those nocturnal visions. Lucid and immersive, my dreams have opened a doorway to another world and exposed my true essence.

As a child, I had been assimilated into the household of a rich, influential, coastal family. I've wanted for nothing in the past sixteen years, having been privy to all the opportunities such wealth can provide; comfort, culture, travel, education.

Yet the revelations of my recent dream-state convey a vastly different account of my life. For within the crystalline depths of that undersea milieu hides an ancient yet secretive race. A race that has forever guarded the treasures of ill-fated shipwrecks and sunken, dead civilizations. A race propagating itself by desperate and, some might say, horrific means.

A race who worship the Elder God himself.

As I crouch naked and shivering among the rocks near the shore, the setting sun illuminates the horizon in fiery red undulations. With the darkening ocean waters stretched out before me and the sandy beach at my back, this wild, rugged coastline is a juncture, a haven, a crossroads of earth, sky, and sea where I can gather my strength and resolve.

To embrace, on this extraordinary All Hallows Eve, my destiny.

#

Samuel and Verity Steadman had acquired me from an orphanage to be raised in privileged seclusion. At least that was the story I'd always been told. My pathetic appearance touched their hearts, they said. I am abnormally large for a girl with slightly bulging eyes, bits of webbed flesh stretched between toes and fingers, a rough scaling of the skin around my neck, a curvature of the spine giving me a minor humpbacked aspect. They rationalized my life would have been more difficult because of my physical deformities, subject to cruelty and derision. They rescued me to live in peace, solitude, and studious and artistic pursuits. What wonderful, caring people they were!

A lie. All a lie.

My father always assured me he'd inherited his wealth. In fact, he had obtained that money in another manner, one which, at first, astonished and disgusted me with its boldness and unnatural carnality.

I discovered the truth in quite ordinary fashion. Being a lonely soul, I had no real friends and spent most of my time in the Steadman's vast, richly-furnished library. There, I perused certain old tomes and ancient scrolls included in their singular, splendid collection. Arcana of the occult, witchcraft, and magic fascinated me, and it was during one of my eager explorations into those forbidden topics when I discovered the origin of my solitary existence.

The journal I found secreted away on top of one of the bookshelves lay covered in dust, apparently discarded and forgotten. Curiosity urged me to peruse its timeworn pages, where within I recognized my adoptive mother's distinctive handwriting. Her accounts of generations of Steadmans engaging in demonology and black magic were not so hard to comprehend considering my own prurient interests, but the true means my father employed to acquire his fortune left me physically ill. I took to my bed, nauseated and repulsed.

Unbelievable as they sounded, the shocking entries would explain much. How could I have been so deaf and blind to such subterfuge?

Not confessing what I'd discerned, I brushed off Verity's attempt to soothe me, telling her I'd developed a severe headache, an affliction I was occasionally prone to. Tossing and turning, I eventually drifted off into a troubled sleep.

The dream-state manifested then, coalescing into extraordinary, kaleidoscopic impressions. Within an ethereal landscape, a figure materialized, shadowy and indistinct, tall and imposing. "We have finally found you, Daughter of the Sea," it whispered in a low, sibilant voice. "Await us when next the moon is full." It gestured with a monstrous hand, one of claw and scale.

I awoke crying out, covered in sweat, gasping for air like a... a fish suffocating on dry land.

That evening I begged off accompanying the Steadmans to a séance in the nearby seaside town of Innsmouth. They left me in the charge of their maid whom I'd always been able to circumvent if I desired. Repelled by my appearance, the woman was quite happy to leave me to my own devices. I never told the Steadmans of their servant's intolerance and lax care. Her disobedient behavior suited my intermittent wayward purposes perfectly.

So it was, with spade in hand and harboring a grim determination, I ventured by waxing moonlight to the Steadman family cemetery. Located a quarter-mile from the main house atop a hill overlooking the ocean, the small group of burial plots lay within splintered darkness. Gravestones and a single above-ground vault sprouted from the ground like abandoned cairns. A chill breeze wafted over the summit, bringing with it the mysterious, tantalizing scents of the sea. Spread before me were the final resting places of the Steadman ancestors.

Except for one.

Though tall, lanky, and fragile-seeming, I was, in fact, quite strong. I'd always wondered why I possessed such an exceptional vigor and, needing to have some secrets of my own, kept that fact hidden. Now, I suspected I knew the reason of it.

I found the unmarked grave described in the lost journal and, gripping the spade firmly, attacked the earth at my feet with a vengeance.

Soon I unearthed a wooden coffin, its rotted lid breaking open easily. With a shudder, I stepped away from the skeletal remains revealed within.

Its frame exceedingly tall, the misshapen skull possessing large eye sockets and long fangs, the clawed feet and hands displaying a fine bony mesh of webbing between fingers and toes, the skeleton appeared both frightening and exhilarating to look upon.

Before me was all that was left of my true birth mother--one of the Deep Ones, those eldritch followers of the Elder God. That knowledge sprang unbidden from some long-suppressed recess of my mind. Awe and wonder enshrouded me.

How can I describe such a revelatory moment? Both glorious and frightening! Samuel Steadman never inherited his wealth. Instead, in a fit of greed and a lust for power, he had made an unholy pact with the Deep Ones. He would conceive one of the hidden race's spawn in exchange for the human treasure sunken beneath the sea.

A product of my father's seed and the gestation within a Deep One's womb, I was that progeny.

But because Verity was barren and hungered to have a family,

Samuel reneged on his promise. After securing the treasure, he betrayed and imprisoned my undersea mother until she had birthed me, then killed her. My adoptive mother's text wasn't clear on why my father hadn't completely disposed of the corpse. Nevertheless, during the ensuing years, I had been successfully concealed and protected, even though my adoptive parents still resided close to the sea, the source of the ancient sea race's power.

Certain entries in Verity's journal had gotten to the heart of that mystery. The Steadmans had developed some dark ability of legerdemain and had been able to counter the power of the Deep Ones with demon magic.

Until now.

I dropped the spade, looked skyward and began to laugh, tears flowing from my protruding eyes. I became intoxicated on the sudden possibilities of my true nature. Only two days more until the full moon, coinciding with All Hallows Eve, and then the world of my dreams would become blessed reality! I no longer feared it.

I reburied my mother and joyously ran back to the Steadman house. It seemed I had waited all of my life to be free. I could wait a little longer.

Besides, one final task demanded my attention.

#

I am here, Daughter of the Sea.

As the voice from my dreams intones inside my mind, a magnificent creature rises from the shallows near the rocks I huddle behind. The surf boils and froths around the Deep One's muscular, green-skinned torso. A momentary fear clutches at my heart, to be replaced by the thrilling anticipation, danger, and excitement I've long been denied.

Silvered moonlight bathes the Deep One in flickering lambency.

I'm afraid if I look away, the glorious sight will vanish like a snuffed candle flame.

Stepping off the rocks into the warm surf to meet my deliverer, I no longer feel alone. I finally have a purpose, a destiny, a community where I can belong.

I, Alana Steadman, no longer exist, if indeed I ever had.

My gore-spattered dress and bloody knife lay in the sand behind me. Samuel and Verity Steadman will never lie to me again. My true mother has been avenged.

The fully-formed gills at my neck pulse and wetly hiss. The small scales on my naked body shimmer in rainbow hues. Reaching out, I take hold of the Deep One's cool, clawed hand as he leads me away from the shore.

To return home at last.

Relentless assault
when we fall, we join their ranks
army of the damned

-Vincent Baverso

DEAD DOG GONE
by Katie Pugh

There were three things Nancy was really good at.

1. Making pancakes.

2. Necromancy.

3. Getting rid of Jehovah's Witnesses. See #2!

It was Halloween, and Nancy had stayed awake binge-watching everything in the "Horror" and "Halloween Favorites" sections of Netflix since October 29th. She got up and immediately spent nine hours getting even more ready for her favorite day, which meant: decking her old house – which was spooky for most of the year anyway – with a fresh coating of spider webs (the ones she put up on October 1 had become sad and unsuitable), adding a few more pumpkins and lastly, putting together her giant cauldron of candy. Which was really her giant cauldron of magicky death that had been cleaned and then filled with candy. This was how it went every year: the kids took candy, she would stay inside and wait for Death.

That's not supposed to sound like an angsty song lyric. She actually waited for Death. The man. Although these days he came around on a motorcycle instead of a pale horse or whatever. This was their night. Tradition. And he was one of the few people who she let come into her house, what with all its questionable elixirs lining the walls and assorted esoterica. Because he got her. So, she pulled her stringy blond hair up, put the yoga pants away and even applied a little bit of lipstick. It felt weird, but it was Halloween. That made it okay.

She heard the deliberate stomps of children coming up the old wooden stairs, murmuring appreciatively about her array of not only Reese's Peanut Butter pumpkins but Reese's Peanut Butter 4-packs. *That's right kids. Take those sugar bombs home to your parents.* And so it went for about a half hour until suddenly the crinkle-crinkle of candy wrappers was interrupted by a blood-curdling scream.

Nancy leapt out of her recliner and ran outside, where a werewolf, a Superman and some Disney princess she didn't recognize were crowded around the cauldron. The screaming was coming from the werewolf, who had grabbed a Caramel Milky Way, only to find something large, furry and…horned on the other end.

"Huh," Nancy said.

The kids ran, and Nancy watched as the ball of fluff with spikes paused momentarily to mark its glorious victory and then ate the Milky Way. In the wrapper. It then turned its liquidy ebony eyes at her and woofed. The puppy with two horns protruding between its two floppy ears danced around in the middle of the candy like she was the best person ever. It was equal parts disturbing and gut-wrenchingly adorable.

She poked one of the horns. There was no sign of it coming off.

She gave it a bit of a yank, and the puppy's pink tongue darted out at her arm.

"Huh," she said again, falling in love dramatically and immediately.

Death showed up on his hog not long after the mysterious cute monster did. He was wearing his favorite black leather jacket, and his black beard had been trimmed. It looked good, and she told him as such. "Come on in. I have something cheap and red, or something cheap and white. You pick."

Death didn't move, and actually looked uncomfortable. She

frowned.

"I actually just came by to say hi. I can't stay this year."

Nancy's frown turned into a full upper-case D.

"I'm sorry--I'm sorry. It's kind of a big deal. There was this incident with some hellhounds and my, uh, management asked me to try and round them up. You haven't seen any weird animals around, have you?"

"I saw a squirrel give me the stinkeye once."

"There is something really wrong with you. Any stray dogs?"

She wanted to say, *like the one in my bathroom? Like the one that I want to keep? Like the one that is unlike all other puppies because it has horns and it's adorable and it eats candy and doesn't die? Like that one?* But she didn't. Instead, she made this strange kind of honking laugh and said, "That's crazy. You're crazy. Whatever, man."

He gave her a big, warm hug before getting back on his motorcycle and driving away into the night. Nancy felt an uncomfortable sticky ball in her stomach. She had done the right thing, right? The puppy would have ended up in Hell. She had heard it was a bad place. Not good for puppies. Ergo, this was a good thing, right? Right?

This will teach you to blow me off, the irrational voice in her head added as she went back inside. Opening the door to the bathroom, the pup came loping out, once again with that look on his black puffball face that said, "I am so glad to see you! Let's eat candy now, please!" She glanced in the bathroom and saw that he had devoured a sealed bag of sanitary napkins and the two rolls of toilet paper from her dispenser. By the end of the night, he somehow also got half of the something cheap and red.

By Christmas, Bentley – she had settled on that, for the classy black car from a book that she liked and how it kind of sounded like a cuter 'Beelzebub' – was the size of a full-grown Newfoundland.

Which was good, because that was the closest to a breed he could really be considered. A great, horned Newfoundland.

When spring rolled around, he was roughly cow-sized. Kind of cow-shaped too, with his girth.

Summer came, and Bentley was really a good name for him because that's what he looked like he had for breakfast with a side of the aforementioned cow and Newfoundland.

He never grew out of his sweet puppy disposition, and luckily he was pretty content to laze around with her every day. She moved most of the furniture out of the house to accommodate the growing dog, and by fall of the next year, he had been given the entirety of the downstairs. Really the only downside to his size was when he had started running in his sleep once and taken out half of a wall. No biggie. She imagined selling the house and boasting about its *open* floor plan.

The food, though, that was the worst part.

Despite how funny it was at first, Nancy didn't like Bentley eating non-food-stuffs. The bigger he got, the more he ate. And the poorer she got.

It was Halloween again before she knew it. She heard the tell-tale rumble of Death's motorcycle coming up the street, and for the first time she felt unsettled. She had to tell him. Well, actually, that wasn't true. There was no way he was going to miss seeing Bentley when he walked in; given that his body now extended from the kitchen into the living room, with the tail somewhere down the hall.

When he came inside the house, Death took off his shades and whistled low. "I love what you've done with the place," he said, his tone flat.

"Thanks. It's all the rage right now. Maximum Mammal. They did a spread on it in Vogue." She had never read Vogue. She hoped he hadn't either.

He rubbed between his eyes. "Nance, you're killing me."

"I didn't know what else to do. He showed up, I took him in, and I just figured…"

"What? That you could take care of him? That it would be just like having a regular dog or something? That he would stop growing? Because they don't. They get bigger and bigger and that's the point. They drag souls and guard the underworld and they are not pets." He had put his hand against Bentley's flank like it was a wall. The floor thudded as the giant tail wagged.

"He wouldn't have been any good for that anyway!" she insisted. "Look at him! He'd rather sleep then drag or guard anything. And he was here, and you weren't." She regretted how typical, how *human*, the words sounded as soon as they came out of her mouth.

"Is that what this is about?"

She didn't say anything.

"Nance. I can't always be here. I mean, it's nice every year to see you but . . . I don't exactly get much of a break, you know?"

She still kept her eyes down.

"So can I take him?"

She looked at Bentley. She thought about the damage to the house, the food money and all the time it had taken away from her studies. She buried her face in his great black mane, trying to hide the tears that were springing up. She shook her head.

Death chewed on his lip for a second. "Look. All my bosses care about is getting the 'hell' out of him and off of Earth. If I take his horns, that should be enough. But he's going to be a normal dog after that. Normal size, normal everything."

"He's going to poop, isn't he."

"Yup."

"Dammit."

"But most importantly," he went on, "he's going to die eventually, Nance. You have to be okay with that."

She let out a little sob.

He rolled his eyes. "He's going to die," he repeated, slower.

She stiffened.

Oh. Oh! She made that horrible honking laugh. "I can deal with that!"

"Yeah, that's what I…"

"Because I have like zero respect for the boundaries of life and death!"

"Stop. Please."

"It will be like that Tim Burton movie. But better. Because I've been doing this way longer than that kid was."

He kissed her on the head. "Have I mentioned there is something seriously wrong with you?" Even as he said it, he was smiling and reaching up to magic away the horns.

They hugged, and even as Bentley began to change, she realized that she wasn't just excited about his ultimate fate as the world's most cuddly zombie dog but that she was excited about the life they had before them, for many Halloweens to come.

Besides, she could always make new horns. She had plenty of bones lying around.

Poet at the wake
mourning with pen and paper
funerary writes

-Vincent Baverso

NEVER THE LESS
NEVER AGAIN
NOT A CHANCE
NEVER FOR A MINUTE
NOT IN THIS LIFE
NO MORE
... DAMN

THE AUTHOR
by Karen Yun-Lutz

Once upon a mid-morn weary, while I pondered bleak and bleary
Over this month's writing challenge chore
While I gulped down coffee bitter, suddenly there came a Jitter
As of some plan idly forming, forming in my foggy gourd
Tis some reverie, I sputtered, 'lurking in my foggy gourd
Only dreams, and nothing more.

Distractedly I remembered who invoked this mad endeavor,
As each verse sought to engender words astute and within stored
And with cogitation did I muster; lots of words with glint and luster
From the depths of mental teaching-reaching for a goal absurd
For the diacritic group whom this scribe has hailed as WorD
Unsung here for evermore.

And the endless thoughts uncertain--left my flustered mind avertin'
Chilled me-killed me with disfigured errors never seen before;
So that words, ripped from my soulless bleeding heart, I sat
repeating
Tis some words upon the paper from my noggins core
Just some words upon the paper from my noggins core
Only a poem, and nothing more.

Soon enough my thoughts grew stronger, indisposed they were no
longer

Words, said I, my prose, surely your quotations I explore
Substantially I was waking, and so quickly I was making
Some plan that was idly forming, forming in my foggy gourd
That I charge was sure attainment--to hidden thoughts unexplored;
Flourish there; a metaphor

Deep into that flourish seeking, hours I sat there, writing, tweaking
Mending, fixing words no author ever dared to write before;
But the words were still so broken, and the paper gave no token
And the only words there spoken, were the bitter words, 'no more!'
This I whimpered, and a sob wailed back the words, 'no more!'-
Narrative rhyme, tis a vast chore

The air around me then grew fragrant, spicy sweet and somewhat
flagrant
When soft gossamer nymph gliding, slipped through my open door
Wench, I cried, which author sent thee - spook or agent spy or
banshee
Thief-thief and mesmerer, to seduce from me what my soul bore
Leave oh leave this addled author and purloin my pen no more
Yawned the imp, tis a snore.

Wordsmith! said she, thing of talk, you omit words, repressed of
shock.
Bolden words scribed, from alluring ancient exotic shore
Enticing to cause contentment, from the sidhe land of
enchantment-
From my home, seductive fleshly- restrain lightly, stifle no more
Is there -is there shame within thy head? Touch me-touch me, I
implore
Quoth the author, temptress whore!

Wordsmith am I, and do not knock-A story void of words of shock

Omitting brazen words impious that from my breath might pour
Shows how this soul remains unblemished, chaste of iniquitous
spore
Depraved words shall not taint my tale, reserved for the prize of
Nobel
Nary shall a smudge tarnish words, reserved for the prize of Nobel
Purity reigns, forevermore!

By these words our way is parting, nymph or wench, I cried
upstarting
Suffer me no longer stranger, leave for a stranger land and shore
Beyond this horizon look for, the door to summer and of yore
Leave my written words untorn- haunt my motivation no more!
Mistress take leave thy harsh light, take leave with you your bold
spoor
Quoth the mistress, I am lore

And the author, never quitting, still is sitting, still is getting
To the pinnacle of germane within this narrative's core;
This limp mind now psychopathic with phantasm visions spastic
As the words bespoken dim now from a mind so torn and sore
Bent these thoughts beyond cognition; twisting logic to frost-hoar
Quoth the author, there is no more.

Serial killer
his pantry stuffed with corpses
closet skeletons

-Vincent Baverso

HELP
WANTED

CONEY HIJINX
by Joe Coluccio

I saw the guy in a rabbit suit. He was at the wheel of a pick-up with a license from just over the state line. *Another damn foreigner,* was what I thought. He pulled over to the curve, hopped out, and went into Sully's Tavern. I waited for a couple more punch lines of a joke to join him. When they didn't show I walked into the bar.

"Hey, Sully, did you see a guy in a rabbit suit come in here?"

"Last booth." Sully indicated with his thumb.

I walked down the line of tables. "Listen," I said to the guy, "can I ask you a question?"

He motioned me to the other side of the booth. Took a long pull from his glass of draft beer.

"I'd like to get a suit like that."

"What?" His voice was cartoon character squeaky.

"You know, for the kids. On their birthday, I mean. I like to come as some kind of a barnyard animal, but the horses and cows need two people and the lion just scares the hell out of 'em."

"It's not a costume."

Definitely peculiar. "What? You're a real rabbit?"

"Not a rabbit." The words kind of warped and warbled then trailed off in a fumbling "t'.

"Buddy," I said," I never thought you was a rabbit."

Then he said it. "I'm a…" (I can only try to spell it and that is after hearing it about a million times) "brrrndig(click)gasvelt. But please just call me Claude."

"Claude the Hopper?" was the only thing I could think to say.

He finished the glass of suds and slapped it down on the table. "You're Rufus?"

Everyone around town knows me. Even Claude the gigantic rabbit.

"Come with me." he said.

I gotta tell you I was reluctant as hell. Not because I was embarrassed to be seen with a rabbit. Hell, people around here who know me would think that was downright normal.

"Where?" I asked.

"Don't you read?" He asked back. "Down the rabbit hole."

Now, my wife says I got more curiosity than sense and when that bunny put the pick-up in gear I admit I got a little, you know, nervous. The truck didn't have no seat belts and the big coney drove like a maniac. I closed my eyes tight when we blew past the stop light at Center and Oak. It turned green. I turned red yellow and green. We headed straight for the block long, high as the trees, brick privacy wall the McAllisters put in two summer's ago. I was on the floor tryin' to pull one giant rabbit foot off the accelerator. We hit it smack dab in the middle, then whizzed through. Claude shifted into overdrive.

He looks down at me. "We go between the mortar joints." says the big dumb bunny.

I climb back up into the passenger seat. "I could use a carrot." I say to him.

"Behind the seat." he says to me.

Out the window the scenery has disappeared and is replaced by black, dark as a sinner's soul. The hare pulls back on the steering wheel and we drop straight down, hood first at about a bezillion miles an hour. Then we turn right. Don't never let it be said that a Ford F-150 doesn't corner well on the plunge. My hands were jammed up against the dash, holding me back into my seat until I passed out.

I awake and a bunch of hopping fiends are holding me over their heads carrying me down a set of massive dirt-dug stairs. We end up in a room that looks kinda like a mud cathedral with all these arches meeting in a point about fifty feet above me. They lay me down on a table. When I try to get up, a bunny with a nasty looking set of hedge clippers shakes his finger back and forth at me. Some music starts. It sounds like that song about Peter Cottontail hopping down the bunny trail played on a bunch of dishes and pans and a bag pipe with a flapping hole in the side. Up pops Claude, the rabbit I met in Sully's. He is in a long, silk, purple robe.

"Don't worry we didn't bring you here to eat you." Until that moment being eaten by some bunny rabbits was about the last thing on my mind. I started looking around for a big stew pot. "We'd like to ask your advice."

"My advice?" *My* advice?

"You work in advertising, do you not?"

"I do not." I say with all honesty. "I work over at the feed store."

"You put together the advertisements for the Green Sheet?"

"Well, yeah. But . . ."

"It is your voice over the loud speaker announcing the sales of the week?"

"Sure, but . . ."

"Then you are involved in advertising?"

"I just sell feed."

"Precisely! We would like you to prepare an ad campaign for our invasion."

"You have an invasion?"

"We'd like to corner the market on fear."

"Fear?" I can't say I was afraid, but there was something a tetch weird about my predicament.

"All Hallows Eve is coming up, right?"

"Can't disagree with you there."

"We live in a hole under the ground, right?"

I look around. "Yeah, it's actually pretty impressive down here."

"But still a hole, right?"

"Yeah okay, right."

"So do moles and worms and a bunch of other creepy creatures. We live in the dark. Like vampires and werewolves and ghosts, a whole host of scary things, right?"

The rabbit with the clippers opens and closes them with a slow menace a couple times. Even though what Claude was saying had more holes than a rabbits warren, I agreed with him. "So?"

"So, we want to terrify people, starting on Halloween."

"You want to terrify little kids with shopping bags in their hands looking for candy?"

"And adults. Then when everyone is cowering in their homes we want to take over the Earth."

"That makes it sound like you guys are some kind of aliens from outer space."

"Not outer space. We are brrrndig(click)gasvelt."

"And you expect me to help you?"

"Or maybe we'll eat you."

We haggled quite a bit, but they made me a pretty good offer. So I quit the feed store. I sit here all day at Sully's with a computer and a cell phone. Take my advice. I wouldn't go out this Halloween, if I was you. Claude and his crew have got these big fangs poking out of the side of their mouths. They're fake looking as hell, but I get paid a good buck to scare you. So, really, stay home. Don't open your door. The boogie man has really big ears.

Child's holiday comes,
You take the time to see me.
So I eat your eyes.

-Douglas Gwilym

HALLOWEEN HAIKU

by Douglas Gwilym

Thing about costumes:
You can never tell for sure
It's human inside.

*

Razor blades do bite,
Slit throats do bleed on clean sheets.
This mask won't come off.

*

I am a mermaid.
I swim and sing to please you.
What sharp teeth I have.

Bob for apples, Dad.
The best one's at the bottom.
Don't come up for air.

*

Trick or treat or burn.
I witched, I watched, they flayed me.
I'll teach tricks to you.

*

Misunderstood Hell.
It wants to warm your bones well.
Aromatic dish.

*

Candy for piggies
Has two special properties:
You oink; and you die.

Woken from sound sleep
toe hits the coffee table
a bump in the night

-Vincent Baverso

ILY JOURNAL
OCT 31ST
oops

IN HIS OWN BLOOD

by Jon Carroll Thomas

I heard the words—spoken aloud from the book and into the sacred artifact—they called to me and I followed. From worlds beyond, I have come, to shed my mantle of smoke and darkness to bow before my new master. For him, I am prepared to wage unholy war, to overthrow gods, to shake all of creation to ruin.

I speak in the language by which I was summoned, "Oh great necromancer, what is your bidding?"

But the man at the desk will not stop writing. He glances up only briefly, eyes wide and bloodshot, and then crouches behind his heaps of yellow parchment to resume his mad scrawl.

I draw nearer and watch the sweat course down his ruddy scalp and drip from his quivering nose, into the pages of his rapidly filling notebook.

"Pardon me . . ." I begin. He cuts me off with an expulsion of inarticulate gibbering.

Now, one thing I cannot abide is a rude necromancer. I force him to look upon me but it is more than his fragile body can take. He shrieks and tumbles apart in my grasp like so much wet sand.

Later, crammed behind his tiny desk, I attempt to make sense of his notes. It all now seems like such a silly misunderstanding. My summoner was only a curious and careless child. And I made such an awful mess of his library. The least I can do, I suppose, is to write this last entry. Whoever reads this, please excuse my handwriting. I could only use my littlest finger to write with, and there was only one thing I could use for ink.

Shambling zombies
the dead returning to life
just Monday morning

-Vincent Baverso

TO BRIDGE THE NIGHT
by Brandon Ketchum

The Betsy Ross Bridge loomed high above Tyler, outlined by the moon, its footing shrouded in gloom. He plodded along beside the Delaware River, sucking air. He'd downed a sixer before heading out, and wanted to clear his head before the party.

He raised his eyes so he didn't stumble around a turn, and found a hot chick in the middle of the path. She was dressed like an-- Edwardo? Victorin? *Victorian*--like a *Victorian* lady. He couldn't see any leg, or make out her shape, but her tits were huge, pushed up by that corset thingie beneath the dress. Tyler couldn't believe his luck.

"Hey, baby, you lost?"

"No, no, I'm merely...looking."

He gave a cocky smirk. "Maybe *I'm* what you're looking for."

She smiled back at him. "Hmm, perhaps."

"Great costume, but you got the hat wrong," he said.

"Oh?"

"Yeah, it's not tiny like Victorian chicks' hats really were in olden days."

"I suppose I'm too old-fashioned for those." She giggled behind her hand.

Tyler laughed along with her, though he had no idea what was so funny.

"Nice pirate costume," she finally said.

"Yeah, thanks." He pulled out his plastic sword and held it near his crotch. "I'm Long Dong Silver. Get it?"

"Are you referencing the villain from Treasure Island?"

"Uh, yeah, sure." He sheathed his pathetic sword.

She turned to continue down the path. Tyler walked beside her, trying to figure out how to get closer without appearing skeevy.

She glanced sideways at him. Her soft blue eyes entranced him. "Do you matriculate nearby?"

"Matricu-what?"

"Study."

"College, right. Yeah, I go to Temple." He paused and had to keep from slapping his forehead. "Say, I'm Tyler. I didn't catch your--"

"Temple? I hear it's a...large school."

"Yeah, it's a banging campus with tons of chicks--I, I mean, students." Again, he wanted to facepalm himself.

"It must be, if it needs so much *parking space*."

"Parking space? That reminds me of this old campus legend. Something about digging up a cemetery for a parking lot or some shit. True story."

"What's true for one is eternal for another," she whispered.

What a weird chica. She was hot, though, so whatever. He went to slip an arm around her waist, but she swished her hips out of reach. Rebuffed, he tried holding hands, but she pulled hers away.

She stepped to the path's edge and beckoned him to join her there. Searching for some way to make progress with the Victorian lady, Tyler gestured at the water, some ten or so feet down the steep bank. "Uh, it's beautiful, huh? The moon. The bridge, the river. You know."

She made a tsking sound. "Oh, you think so, do you?"

"Hey, uh, did I say something wrong?" he asked.

"This bridge is an abomination with a grim foundation."

He shrugged. "Traffic would be killer without it."

She continued as if he hadn't spoken. "And your masters at Temple are the philistines who provided the *material* it was built upon."

Tyler hunched away from her and averted his eyes, readying a brush-off. "Look, lady, it's getting late, and I got a party to get to, so..."

Something hit him in the back, sending him over the edge. Tyler toppled down the bank. Hit his head on something hard. Banged his knee, twisted an ankle. He crashed to a stop on the rocks in the shallows. His back throbbed. He coughed, spit out water, groaned, and tried to regain focus. The Victorian lady was there. She knelt in the water, looming above him.

"Wha...?"

She grabbed his hair and twisted his head around so he was face to face with one of the river rocks. His neck strained agonizingly. "Look at it!" she screamed. "*Look at it!*"

Dazed, and in a lot of pain, Tyler tried to focus on the flat chunk of dark stone. "W-What am I supposed to...?"

Figures glowed green on the stone, showing letters and numbers he hadn't been able to see in the dark. On top it said "*en Gervis*," and below it was "*3-1897.*"

Tyler felt his strength returning; his head cleared. He was in some seriously weird shit. With a bellow he thrust away from the Victorian lady--well, he tried to, anyway. She held him on his back with one lone hand in the center of his chest. He squealed and struggled to slip free, but she held him firm.

The Victorian lady dropped her eyes to his, eyes that had turned black as death's robes. Tyler wanted to bury himself to avoid those eyes. To his relief, her preternatural gaze slid away and rested on the stone. "Allen Gervis, with this sacrifice I summon thee, to avenge thyself on our nemeses."

Tyler shrieked, bucked and rolled his hips, straining every muscle to escape, succeeding only in disturbing the water. Other letters and numbers glowed beneath the rippling black surface.

The Victorian lady reached into the water and hefted out a large stone. The glowing letters read "Helena Thatcher." With the jagged rock broken off below, it looked as if the name had been nibbled at by stony teeth. She pressed this onto Tyler's chest and forced his hands around it. He recoiled at her freezing touch, and the cold stone, yet for some reason he clutched it tight.

Tyler's legs jerked, his stomach lurched, and he found himself standing and facing out toward the river. Then he took a step forward, water up to his knees, and another. He fought to clench his leg muscles, to stay in place, but was unable to stop himself from taking another step, going waist deep.

"Now can I go home," she said behind him, her sighing voice a satisfied moan that freaked the living hell out of him. "Now can I rest."

Tyler sank into the shallows, screaming his terror. The river flooded his mouth, cutting him off. Trying to breathe water, he sank into the depths, then sank deeper, deeper than the river itself.

Witches use old brooms
yet angels use wings to fly
Who's the real monster

-Vincent Baverso

THE SANDBOX SINGULARITY

by Thomas Sweterlitsch

I.

Reggie, he was once called, years ago when he was a bookkeeper, sometimes *Reg the Edge* by the warehouse crew because he'd been pudgy and jovial back then. Reggie was lean now, and sinewy, the thinnest he'd ever been. The crown of his head was bald but his hair grew lustrous and dark otherwise, hanging well past his shoulders. His beard was thick, his mustache too. He stepped outside his shed to relieve himself and begin his calisthenics routine. Stretches, jumping jacks, stretches, squats. Reggie was a good runner—unusually stable despite the slight ligament tear and hernia. Where other organics had rent and split apart, eventually succumbing to the years of running, Reggie remained intact.

Some other runners were congregating now, stepping from their sheds and lean-tos to relieve themselves, or wandering over from who knows where, beginning their own calisthenics routines. Everyone was naked, skins mottled by burning particulates in the air or from having been caught out in acidic sprays of rain. Reggie surveyed the field. He recognized most of the other runners, though some were new—that pale one was here again, that lanky pale one who annoyed Reggie so much, for no real reason he annoyed Reggie, just because his skin was milky white and freckled and his reddish hair was long and when he ran he loped with an odd forward momentum. The pale one was a good runner, though, Reggie had to admit, but look at him; rolling his neck, *crack, crack,* those knee thrusts and hamstring stretches, *one, two, one, two,* extending his arms out to his side, rolling them like a bizarre white bird flapping featherless wings.

There were about three dozen runners gathered this morning and once the short one with the corkscrews of dark hair started running, everyone else started running also. Reggie sprinted at full tilt. All the other runners sprinted too, but most couldn't keep pace for long, falling behind, wheezing. Maybe they'd never run before, beginners reassigned here from other duties because they'd somehow shown promise, or maybe they simply weren't cut out for running and were placed here so they would wear out more quickly than if they stayed in other, more sedentary tasks. Some would get better with each passing day and become respectable runners in their own right, but others would collapse, dead or left to die. This morning there were only seven or eight real contenders to accumulate the most laps and actually win the day. Strictly speaking, younger runners who could outpace Reggie in wind sprints and distance runs were common, but Reggie held his own. He always held his own. He rarely won these races, but his endurance was incredible—a miracle of the flesh. He was still a runner long after some of the greatest had injured themselves and were allowed to expire.

Reggie *ran,* high-stepping through weeds and bramble; sprinting through the narrow alleys between disintegrating buildings, gathering pure speed once he reached the main streets and the smooth concrete straightaways. His body responded, surging with happiness, a runner's high. When he rounded the pit, there were only four people keeping pace with him. The short one with the corkscrew hair was far ahead of the field, but the annoying pale one was falling behind, and the blonde one, too, another good runner. The rest of the field was still clumped together, just now passing the dead oak tree that marked the first turn. Reggie kicked a little harder, thinking maybe he could catch the short one as they ran along the boardwalk, or maybe through the sand of the shore. The ocean was rust colored and stinging—nothing he'd want to immerse in—but the foraging gulls were circling in the wind and Reggie felt like the gulls must feel, free and happy, happy, happy.

Reggie's happiness intrigued the Mother. One of the Mother's Observers fluttered down from the Mother's belly and floated just behind Reggie's skull, scanning and prying for the particular cause of Reggie's burst of happiness.

Ah, so that was it: a residual memory, a *childhood* memory, the Observer soon discovered. Reginald had been seven years old, had joined a community race—he'd sprinted then just like he sprinted now, on a Saturday morning in a church field, around a track that had been constructed of orange cones. He'd outpaced the other children and won that morning—a shock to both him and his mother who'd watched from the finish line, his victory a complete surprise. An awards ceremony followed, and after Neapolitan ice cream squares served in Styrofoam bowls, he walked in front of everyone to have his hand shaken and receive a plaque, a dark wood mount with a reflective blue plate etched not only with his name but the words *1st Place.* Reggie remembered the dull applause, bitter and cursory clapping from the children who hadn't won and their parents.

The Mother's Observer took this information in. Should we absorb this memory? it asked. Yes, we suppose we should, replied the Mother—and as quickly as the Mother had made this decision, the Observer radiated Reggie's brain, sponging away the memory and adding it to their growing bank of motivations and pleasures. This fine memory, like most of Reggie's other memories, was gone. Reggie stumbled but regained his footing and kept running. He was less happy than he'd been a few moments ago, but content nonetheless. The gulls still circled, it was a temperate mid-morning with low humidity and although the winds that pushed in from over the ocean smelled like decaying meat, they created a nice breeze, pleasant to run in.

Reggie sprinted through the lot of rusted out cars and the gathering of sheds and lean-tos and towards the dead oak tree that marked the first turn. He was about to lap some of the slower runners.

II.

Dusk. The changing light signaled to Reggie that the sprinting imperative would soon ease in favor of the resting imperative, when all runners would cease in their track and jog back to their sheds or lean-tos to mark out their number of laps completed and wait out the storms. Reggie pushed himself harder in these final hours, hoping to eke out another lap or maybe even two, hoping to catch that short runner with the corkscrew hair before the day's running was done.

Reggie turned at the copse of scrub edging the boardwalk onto the long stretch of shore, his feet sinking in sand with each step so he had to practically march as he ran, to keep pace with the shorter runner. He had closed the gap since morning—the shorter runner was faster than Reggie on the straightaways through the town and along the boardwalk, those smooth surfaces, but his shorter limbs betrayed him through the scrub and here in the sand, and with each lap Reggie was able to close the gap a little more, to make up lost time from those straightaways. Reggie had no doubt he would eventually overtake the short runner if the race were an infinite loop—he was close enough now to see the shorter runner's back muscles rippling and smell the sweat perfuming the corkscrew hair.

High step, high step. Reggie drew alongside the shorter runner and kicked to pull ahead when he heard his knee snap and he crumpled to the hot sand startled, screaming. He grabbed his knee. The short runner with corkscrew hair continued running and soon turned from the beach onto that last stretch bordered with Sumac and disappeared from view. Reggie was scared but the sprinting imperative consumed him and so despite the radiating shivers of pain he pulled himself up and tried to run. After two steps, however, the tendons rent apart and Reggie collapsed a second time, the pain so bright that he vomited. The sprinting imperative faded.

Over the years, Reggie had seen other runners whose bodies had failed them, bodies collapsed here on the sand, or tangled in the scrub or laid out on the straightaways. Reggie always ran around them, concentrating on his laps, but once he'd been startled to see several bodies on the beach at dusk crawling toward the ocean, leaving trails through the glistening sand in their wake.

The Mother positioned itself over Reggie, floating into his field of vision. Like a blimp or a blimp-sized jellyfish, Reggie thought, but less distinct than a jellyfish—the Mother was more like a pool of silvery jelly or a hovering lake of mercury. When the storm winds gusted, the Mother's skin rippled and the veins that threaded the silver stood out in starker relief.

An Observer detached itself from somewhere in the Mother's skin, fluttering down to linger just a few inches in front of Reggie. Observers were smallish, reminding Reggie of basketballs, if basketballs could hover—but there was something loathsome about them, something unnatural and repellent. The eye was a glass lens but the shell was leathery and every piece was held together by gluey strings of gristle and rings of fatty beige. Observers were moist and the sound of their breathing sounded like sloshing fluids and they dripped liquid that looked like oily blood. Something *clicked* from somewhere deep in the Observer's shell and Reggie heard a low-pitched hum. Within moments, the pain in his knee diminished.

"Thank you," said Reggie.

Reggie fully expected to stand and run, whether his knee was structurally destroyed or not, leaving him confused when the sprinting imperative failed to resonate.

"What now?" he asked the Observer.

The fetid ocean wind grew stronger, the dusk deepened into a darker shade of violet. Reggie had been so accustomed to the imperatives of sprinting and resting, one imperative following the other in a cycle as certain as night and day, that when a new imperative filled him the sensation was painful, like a gloved hand squeezing sensitive organs. The new imperative was to speak.

"Well, we never had children of our own," said Reggie, "so I suppose I tend to think of the moment I first saw her, my wife—I was older already and she was in college, 8 years between us. She worked at a café. I was wildly attracted to her, nervous whenever she took my order. I was surprised she would even speak to me, but later on she told me that she'd always been attracted to older men."

The Observer clicked, the Observer hummed.

Reggie spoke: "Or this was years later, when Jeanne and I were at the beach, the one in El Segundo, and there were girls showering together, washing sea salt and sand from themselves under those outdoor spigots. Hardly wearing anything at all, and even though Jeanne was beside me, walking right there with me, infuriated that I was looking at those girls, I couldn't help but stare…"

Click, hum—the memory of the shower on the beach was sponged away. The stars were like flares and the Mother was luminescent in the growing darkness. The winds whipped harder and ocean spray burned Reggie like he'd been spritzed with boiling water. He looked into the Observer's camera-eye. He felt another squeeze, that imperative to speak.

"I was young, four or five, maybe younger, and my mother had taken me with her, I can't exactly remember where, the Y, maybe, maybe for swimming classes or aqua yoga, I can't remember, but we were at the pool. I was young enough that she couldn't just let me wander in the hallway so she brought me into the locker room with her. Chlorine. Do you know the smell of chlorine? It's very specific. My mother's friend was with her, Miss McClure, and they undressed in front of me, thinking I was too young to care, but I felt like something ruptured and melted inside me when I saw Miss McClure naked. I had a dream about Miss McClure, that she invited me to touch her but when she revealed herself her body was covered with hair."

Click, hum—the memory was sponged away. The Observer

floated upward like a lost balloon and rejoined the skin of the Mother. Reggie watched as the Mother floated away, roiling across the stormy wind. *Why?* he might have asked himself, but he was filled with a new imperative—nothing painful, this imperative, but a sensation of exhaustion, of thoroughness, of a desire to rupture and melt inside. Reggie rolled onto his stomach and crawled, towing himself along with his hands and elbows, pushing with his good leg, his damaged limb limp and useless. He crawled toward the ocean where he would pull himself into the water, where dissolving tides would eventually wash him to oblivion.

He was in no hurry.

The runner with the blonde hair made his final turn to sprint along the shore—once a rival, Reggie thought this runner was magnificent now, his tanned muscles taut and flexing beautifully as he leapt over Reggie's prone body effortlessly and in stride. Reggie wept for the beauty of the runner, for the beauty of *running*. He continued to crawl. His hand touched the edge of the ocean and despite the corrosive pain he reached forward and pulled himself deeper into the churning water. Another runner made the final turn to sprint along the shore—the pale one, running headlong through the sand with that annoying forward lope, almost galloping, losing himself to that forward heaving momentum, his eyes as certain as death and just as meaningless.

ETYMOLOGY OF WORD

by Diane Turnshek

It started, as all good ideas do, as a "what if?" I had written a story, my first-ever, if you don't count the Christmas puppy story I wrote as a tween. I knew about critique groups for science fiction and fantasy, because Mary Soon Lee had started the Pittsburgh Worldwrights in October of 1993 after asking for my help selecting the participants. I wasn't ready to join her group at that time. Some of the lucky people who had the chance to be in that professional group were: Ken Chiacchia, Flonet Biltgen, Robert L. Nansel, Timons Esaias, Tom Byers, Barton Paul Levenson, Chris Ferrier and Elizabeth Penrose. By the time I finished my story, Mary already had her perfect number, ten members and put me on a wait list. I'm not that good at waiting. What if . . . ?

At the now-defunct South Hills Border's Bookstore, I put up a bold sign in the window (with the manager's okay) that read, "Science Fiction and Fantasy Writers, Meet Here!" with a time and date two months into the future. I figured I'd find some aspiring writers who wanted to join me and then I'd start my own crit group. Or at least, I would have some fun conversations with anyone who showed up. I did not expect what actually happened.

I was late (no surprise to anyone who knows me). I walked onto the upper floor with John Schmid, both of us carrying shopping bags of shiny binders full of printed short story market guidelines, and Parsec and Confluence advertisements. All eyes were on us as we descended the curved central staircase. The fireside lounge was packed! I'd underestimated the number of people who would find my sign intriguing. Professional writers curious enough to show up included William H. Keith, Jr, William Tenn (Phil Klass) and John DeChancie. No one had guessed what the sign was all about. It became an impromptu party (the best kind). At around forty people, the crowd was too large to start one group, so we split and started two, Write or Die on the east side of the city and the Pittsburgh Southwrites to the southeast.

Southwrites began meeting in 1997 at people's houses every other Sunday afternoon. Some of the early members were Barb Carlson, Ann Cecil, Randy Hoffman, John Branch, Chetan Chothani, Judy Friedl, Henry Tjernlund, Jamie Chew, Steve Chew, Mary Turner, Diane McCarty, Larry Ivkovitch and Lynn Hawker. It was social and friendly, open to all and served to bring new writers into the Parsec SF/F/H organization (co-founded by Ann Cecil and Barb Carlson). Many Southwrites members were actively selling stories. The group had a good long run and forged deep friendships, but lost cohesion after Ann Cecil passed away in 2011.

The first meeting of Write or Die (which shortens to WorD) was at Tom Rafalski's parent's house in Irwin in December of 1996. I remember Bill Keith folding himself into a small space in the living room next to the Christmas tree and Tom's mom serving us cookies. We obviously needed a bigger spot, so we shifted to the Monroeville Library (still with candy and cookies).

The WorD group met every-other Tuesday night at the slightly odd hour of 6:45 pm, since that's when I could get there after handing the kids off to a babysitter. There was never a thought of canceling a meeting – we met through snow, rain, heat and gloom of night. Once the library flooded a foot deep and we were herded through the water and out the back door. Several of us saw our first instance of ball lightning as it hit the building, and then we sat in the dark and finished critiquing.

My story was critiqued and I edited it. Then, I brought it back to the group for more comments, because that's what I thought you did. Kevin Geiselman pushed an envelope and a stamp across the table at me. That was his whole critique. I got the message and sent it to Analog Magazine, the longest running science fiction monthly magazine in the world. My first written story was my first sale and my first pro sale, all in one ("Dancing in the Light" Analog Magazine, Dec. 1999).

For years, we met in a back part of the stacks, then, in November of 2001, a new, windowed conference room was added up front. It fit us perfectly, as though it was designed just for us. There were always about forty people on the WorD Yahoo group list, but only a random subset of those showed up at meetings, fifteen or so each time. I didn't care for the stringent rules that some writers groups had in place. WorD had no dues, no limits on length of work or time for crit delivery, how often a member had to show up, or what percentage of the manuscripts had to be critiqued. In order to get on the mailing list, people had to first show up in person at a meeting. We held to Clarion rules, began with the longest story first and went round the circle counterclockwise starting at the author's right. This inclusivity and openness gave us a steady flux of writers through the group. I wanted WorD to always be free and open to the public, and, in that, it perfectly matched the library's rules.

People in the group shared their life stories. We started heading out to a restaurant after the critiques, really getting to know each other. Friendships were made, and some broke hard. I had to kick out one silent guy who had been coming for years, after he turned in an unreadable story with no redeeming qualities, just graphically depicted rape and snuff scenes. We added a rule – no gratuitous violence.

The critiques were impressive–and not just what you'd get in a traditional writing class, like syntax, plot, agency, word choice, style, voice, character development and pacing. Someone always knew when pockets were invented, what the tensile strength of a Mercedes hood was and where the moon would be located in the sky thousands of years in the future. Several people turned their crits into performance pieces and tried to outdo each other by using actual swords to stage the battle scenes as they were written, along with a running critical commentary. One member routinely showed their latest artistic nude model photography during the meetings. One member brought a six-foot long hand to a meeting. It was never dull. We all learned to be better critiquers and better writers.

A writing retreat in cabins in the beautiful Maryland Cumberland Gap National Historical Park bonded us over shared food, company and gaming. Walks in the woods solidified our cosmic perspective and shared love of the genre, even among its myriad facets.

I started Parsec's annual themed Triangulation anthology in 2003 as a way for Pittsburgh genre writers to get a view from the other side of the desk. Most of the editors came from the ranks of WorD members (aside from me, editors and assistant editors included Joseph Benedetto, Pete Butler, Bill Moran, Jamie Lackey, Frank Oreto and Douglas Gwilym). We read slush until patterns emerged. What *not* to do became obvious, if what to do was still not one hundred percent clear.

WorD had writing successes along the way. Some fine writers honed their craft at our table. The ultimate goal was always publication, but limited to science fiction, fantasy and horror. Dozens of novels went through the group and hundreds of short stories. We critiqued poetry, synopses, outlines and cover letters – whatever was needed to get published. Sometimes successes were measured in personal fulfillment and connection, still valued and valuable.

As sometimes happens, life takes over and the WorD group started to sputter. Many people cited home, work and illnesses for the reasons they were not able to write and submit stories or attend meetings. Life got busy. People moved away. Finally, Tracey Levino and I were about the only ones left and the WorD group stalled completely. The last meeting at the Monroeville library was held on June 6, 2011. And on June 21st Tracey, hosted a WorD send-off party at her home.

We're fortunate that Eljay's Used Books (now Rickert and Beagle Books) opened their doors for us. The WorD group is still alive.

But that's a story for Kevin and Karen to tell.

BIOS

Alphabetically

Michael Arnzen (A Check-up for Mr. Bangles) gorelets.com, teaches full-time in the MFA in Writing Popular Fiction program at Seton Hill University, and has been publishing sick and funny horror for about twenty-five years. He holds four Bram Stoker Awards and is author of the novels, Grave Markings and Play Dead. You can catch up with "the best of Arnzen" in the recent re-release of his Bram Stoker Award-winning collection, Proverbs for Monsters from Dark Regions Press. Look for his series, "55 Ways I'd Prefer Not To Die," in The Year's Best Hardcore Horror in 2017.

Vincent Baverso (Assorted Haiku) holds a degree in English writing from the University of Pittsburgh. A true Renaissance man, Vincent loves to create. He is a draftsman, poet, philosopher, carpenter, pipe maker, artist and mead maker. He does all this when he's not working on his latest novel or spending time with his wife and three children.

Joe Coluccio (Coney Hijinx) is President of Parsec, Pittsburgh Premier Science Fiction and Fantasy Organization. He has been involved with science fiction in some manner since the third grade in elementary school. He was program director for WYEP-FM, a local community access radio station in the first years of its existence and worked as a traffic manager for a television production studio. He currently teaches courses for the Osher Long Life Learning Institute at the University of Pittsburgh on subjects including science fiction and noir literature.

Douglas Gwilym (Halloween Haiku) Douglas Gwilym is a writer and editor who has also been known to compose a weird-fiction rock opera or two. If you aren't lucky enough to have caught him performing his stories and music at venues around Pittsburgh, you can find him at douglasgwilym. bandcamp.com or follow him on twitter at @douglasgwilym

Kevin M. Hayes (A Story Book Halloween) hates writing biographies for books in which his stories appear. For some, he relies on humor to entertain his readers; in others, he keeps to the serious side of his personality, hinting at dark, forbidden things readers would be best kept unaware of. Some of his stories and, by extension, his biographies have appeared in "Six From Parsec" and the first two volumes of "Triangulation." Kevin has also published limericks, but doesn't expect you to believe that. Sometimes, he reads for the podcast, "Pseudopod." You will have to decide whether this is a humorous, or a serious biography.

Larry Ivkovich's (From The Deep) speculative fiction has been published in over twenty online and print magazines. He has been a finalist in the L. Ron Hubbard's Writers of the Future contest and was the 2010 recipient of the CZP/Rannu Fund award for fiction. Published novels include urban fantasy The Sixth Precept and Warriors of the Light (IFWG Publishing).

Brandon Ketchum (To Bridge the Night) is a speculative fiction writer working out of Pittsburgh, PA. He has attended the Cascade Writers Workshop, the In Your Write Mind Workshop, and the Nebulas. His stories have appeared in the anthology MASHED: The Culinary Delights of Twisted Erotic Horror, in Perihelion: the online science fiction magazine, and in the Mad Scientist Journal and other publications.

Frank Oreto (A Walk in the Park) is a writer and editor of weird fiction whose work has appeared in numerous publications including Pseudopod, Fantasy Scroll Magazine and Triangulation. When not writing he can be found cooking elaborate meals for his wife and three perpetually hungry children. You can check up on what he's working on (both stories and food) by following him on Twitter @FrankOreto

Katie Pugh (Dead Dog Gone) wants to live in a world where everybody is a little mad. Katie's work has been featured online and in print, including in the Pittsburgh City Paper, Gadchick.com, Every Day Fiction, Airplane Reading and Moon Magazine. She also frequently muses on her blog, bohemianonrye.com. She has penned two books: a Young Adult urban fantasy novel, Cape and Dagger, and a poetry chapbook, Pickled Miracles, both available on Amazon and through major and local booksellers. When she's not putting words together in a fancy way, you can find her spending time with her husband, making art, taking pictures and adventuring. There's nothing she won't try at least once.

Tom Sweterlitsch (The Sandbox Singularity) is the author of the novels 'The Gone World' and 'Tomorrow and Tomorrow.' He lives in Pittsburgh, PA.

Jon Carroll Thomas (In His Own Blood) is a part-time writer, full-time husband/father, and former Pittsburgher living in Raleigh, NC. He likes scary stories and lives by the mantra, "It's always Halloween somewhere." He has published stories with Zoetic Press and Great Old Ones Publishing and, under the pen name Jonas Moth, with Martian Migraine Press and Dunham's Manor Press.

Diane Turnshek (Etymology) Diane Turnshek teaches astronomy at the University of Pittsburgh and Carnegie Mellon University. She writes science fiction stories with an eye to the stars. She has been on the Board of Directors for both SFWA and Parsec. She taught college writing classes at CMU and St. Vincent and, for nine years, worked as a faculty mentor for grad students at Seton Hill's MFA Writing Popular Fiction program. In Pittsburgh, she is the founder of WorD, a writing and critique group, Alpha, a teen writing workshop, the CMU-Parsec YA Lecture Series and Triangulation, a yearly anthology of speculative fiction.

Karen Yun-Lutz (The Author) Is a mother to five children, an author, photographer, graphic designer, videographer and video editor. She obtained her black belt in Tang Soo Do Karate at the age of fifty-two and studies the Korean sword martial art, Hai Dong Gumdo. For her day job she works part time as a marketing agent and customer service rep for a print company. She spends her free time co-organizing the Write or Die (WorD) writing and critique group and working as the director of public relations for Confluence, the Pittsburgh, PA SF/F/H literary, music and art conference. This is her first go as an editor for an anthology. She had her first story, The Minds I, published in the 2006 Parsec Ink Triangulation anthology. She also has written and published stories and a novel under her pen name. And yes, she is just a tad on the "not quite right" side of the mental health spectrum. But you probably already guessed that if you read the foreword.

Cover Artists

Rhonda Libbey (Cover artist - Yellow King in Carcosa) is an Imaginative Realism artist and illustrator. She live in Pittsburgh Pennsylvania with her wonderfully supportive boyfriend and three silly ferrets. She began her artistic journey when she was 6 years old; beginning with drawing, and has never stopped. An artist is the only thing she ever wanted to be. She has been a professional illustrator and graphic designer since 1996 and has had the good fortune to work on some cool projects and has shown her artwork in some great galleries. Her most recent works are created traditionally in oil paint and gold leaf, with oil paint layered in glazes on top of the metal to achieve a luminous effect. She is drawn to the contrasts of delicate and bold that both oil paint and gold leaf possess.

Nancy Farmer: (Back cover artist - Demons dancing) is a professional artist living and working in the South West of England, a place rich in folklore, both real and invented after a lot of cider. What interests her most is the human form, and the way the gesture and body language of figures can be given a narrative simply through their movement and posture. Since getting into open water swimming she now more commonly paints swimmers rather than fairies and devils, but the subjects are remarkably similar: there is much human form on display, much humour and narrative, and much silliness. You can find her recent work at: www.waterdrawnart. com and her older work at: www.nancyfarmer.gallery

ACKNOWLEDGEMENTS

Profuse and unending thanks to Chris (Rickert) Pluto, the owner of Rickert and Beagle bookstore. You give us the room to exercise our imaginations, hone our craft and launch our dreams.

Thank you to Mark H. Leighty, for your continual support. You are what makes friendship exceptional.

Thank you to the authors for trusting me with your treasured words.

Thank you to Kevin M. Hayes, for being my second set of eyes and in-house artist. I couldn't have done this without you and your support.

Thank you to every backer who donated to our fundraiser. Your generosity is appreciated beyond words.

And thank you, dear reader. You are what makes this book worthwhile.

End of the party
the guests are all going home
dearly departed

-*Vincent Baverso*

We hope you enjoyed reading our first Write or Die anthology,
Knee Deep in Little Devils.
As a thank you for purchasing the print edition we are giving you a code to
unlock special content only available with purchase of the print book.

Special content includes a second ending to "A Storybook Halloween."
Use the QR code below to unlock the content,
or visit: https://word-pgh.weebly.com/kdldspecialcontent.html